PRINCESS
FOR A DAY

Author – P. Tomar

Illustrated by – Giulia Iacopini

In loving memory of my parents, Narendra and Virendra.
I miss you everyday.
-P.Tomar

To my family, Babbo Patrizio, Mamma Simona, and my
little sister Allegra. Thank you for always being there for me.
(and for buying me cereal!)
Giulia. Iacopini

Printed and bound in China

ISBN 978-1-7327528-2-5 (Hardcover)

https://www.PenMagicBooks.com

PenMagic Books provides special discounts when
purchased in larger volumes for premiums and promotional
purposes, as well as for fundraising and educational use.
Custom editions can also be created for special purposes.
In addition, supplemental teaching material can be
provided upon request.

By being yourself,
you put something
wonderful in the
world that was not
there before.

-Edward Elliot-

One night, Bina Trunk watched a show about a princess.

The princess sang,

"I am a royal princess.
I wear a silky gown.
To serve the royal princess,
just bow before my crown!"

The next morning, Bina found Mama Trunk's red silk scarf and tied it around her neck. She rummaged through her costume chest and found a sparkly crown and a pair of glittery shoes.

"Oh wow! I look like a real Princess!"

While coming down for breakfast,
Bina announced,

"I am a royal princess.
 I wear a silky gown.
 To serve the royal princess,
 just bow before my crown!"

Mama Trunk, Papa Trunk, and her brother Babu Trunk giggled and they all bowed to Bina.

"Absolutely, Princess Bina," said Papa Trunk. "Please honor us by having breakfast with us."

Mama Trunk said, "Princess Bina, look, I picked your favorite berries."

After breakfast, Babu and Bina
walked to Grandma Trunk's tea shop.

Bina announced,

"I am a royal princess.
I wear a silky gown.
To serve the royal princess,
just bow before my crown!"

Grandma Trunk smiled, bowed to Bina, and said, "Indeed, Princess Bina, welcome to my little tea shop. How can I be of service?"

Bina replied, "Princess Bina would like some dessert." Grandma Trunk said, "Then I will serve the princess my special milk cake."

"Mm... delicious. The princess is pleased. Tell me, what do you need? I'm a princess and I have treasures."

Grandma Trunk chuckled.
"If Princess Bina could water my herb
garden, that would be very helpful."

Bina replied, "Oh golly! I am a princess, and if I
water the garden my special princess clothes will
get dirty. Besides, princesses don't do little things."

"Come on, Babu," said Bina, "Let's go see what
Grandpa Trunk is doing in his laboratory."

In Grandpa Trunk's laboratory,
Bina announced,

"I am a royal princess.
I wear a silky gown.
To serve the royal princess,
just bow before my crown!"

"Of course, Princess Bina," said Grandpa Trunk. "What an honor to have you visit my laboratory. How can I serve you?"

Princess Bina said, "I want you to make a rocket ship for me to fly to the moon."

"Sure, Princess Bina, but that will take many years of work. However, I have something special for you. I recently made these robotic wings which can make you fly. Would you like to try them?"

Bina didn't hesitate to try out the wings.

"I'm flying! I'm flying! Look at me, Grandpa Trunk! Everyone looks so tiny from up here."

After coming down, Bina followed
Grandpa Trunk to his laboratory.
"The princess is pleased," she said.
"Tell me, what do you need? I have
many treasures!"

Grandpa Trunk smiled.
"If Princess Bina could help
arrange my books that would
be very helpful."

"Oh golly! I am a princess and princesses don't do petty things." Bina turned and left Grandpa's laboratory.

Soon after, their neighborhood friends, Hari Hippo and
Honey Hippo, stopped by to play with Babu and Bina.

Bina sang,

"I am a royal princess.
 I wear a silky gown.
 To serve the royal princess,
 just bow before my crown!"

Hari Hippo and Honey Hippo giggled and bowed to Bina.

Meanwhile, Babu grabbed the garden hose.

Babu sprayed his friends. He soaked Hari Hippo.
Honey Hippo rolled in the mud. They laughed
and splashed and got ridiculously muddy.

Bina looked down at her pretty clothes.
She thought about what a princess would do.
She said, "I want to play, too! Let's play
something a princess can play."

Babu Trunk laughed.
"But Princess Bina, we're not royal!
We don't have treasures. We like
to help, we like to play, and we
love to roll in the mud."

Tears streamed down Bina's cheeks. Looking at her friends having so much fun, she felt left out.

Bina thought and thought. And then she removed her glittery crown, sparkly shoes, and red silk cloak.

"I don't want to be a Princess anymore. I want to play in the mud with my friends."

Bina splish-splashed through the water giggling. "This is more fun than being a princess."

After playing for a while, Bina stopped and hung her head. "I wasn't a good elephant as a princess. I didn't help Grandma Trunk and Grandpa Trunk."

Babu Trunk jumped up. "You still can!"

Bina ran toward the herb garden, filled a can, and watered the plants. She clapped with joy when she saw Grandma's roses bloom.

Grandma Trunk smiled and gave Bina a warm hug.

After she finished watering the plants, Bina ran to see Grandpa Trunk. She helped him arrange his books. Babu Trunk and their Hippo friends helped too.

Honey Hippo said, "Look at this! Grandpa Trunk wrote this book. He's the coolest."

Bina loved being a princess, but then she realized it was more fun being **kind** and being **herself**.

Thank You
for Reading!

If you and your child enjoyed this book, please leave a review on Amazon!
Support Authors -
Read and Review!

Another book on the series:
Babu and Bina at the Ghost Party!
Order your signed copy now @
www.PenMagicBooks.com

acknowledgments

Thank you to everyone who made this book possible!

Nishka Tripathi, Giulia Iacopini, Debbie Manber Kupfer,
Tamara Rittershaus, Bhuvanesh Tomar, Josiah Davis,
Carin-Ann Anderson, Rajat Tripathi, Jay Miletsky, Sherry H,
Katya Bowser, Collen Bruneti, Kaitlyn Sanchez, Sophie Juliet,
Jonathan Gunson, Laurie Wright, Kelly Grettler, Bob Teffek,
Sheri Wall. Kelly Pozniak, Colleen Brunneti.

about the author

Mother, author and animation industry veteran, P.Tomar loves creating short stories for children based on adventure, magic and mythology. Each story is filled with her passion for life, her love of family, and art. Through her character's adventures, she wants to encourage children to pursue their dreams and live life passionately.

To book P.Tomar for a speaking engagement and to see her upcoming book titles, please visit:

https://www.PenMagicBooks.com

about the illustrator

Giulia is a concept artist and illustrator from Rome. Her main inspirations are the warm and sunny colors that surrounded her during her childhood. She tries to give life to her illustrations with magical and happy atmospheres and characters. Her main goal is to inspire other kids through her art, the same way so many artists have done and keep doing!

https://www.GiuliaIacopini.net/